STANDING TALL
Mystery
Series

W9-BIK-281

MULTICULTURAL READERS
SET 1

THE HOWLING HOUSE

ANNE SCHRAFF

Artesian *Press*

P.O. Box 355 Buena Park, CA 90621

STANDING TALL MYSTERY SERIES
MULTICULTURAL READERS
SET 1

Don't Look Now or Ever	1-58659-084-7
Audio Cassette	1-58659-094-4
Audio CD	1-58659-266-1
Ghost Biker	1-58659-082-0
Cassette	1-58659-092-8
Audio CD	1-58659-265-3
The Haunted Hound	1-58659-085-5
Cassette	1-58659-095-2
Audio CD	1-58659-267-X
The Howling House	**1-58659-083-9**
Cassette	**1-58659-093-6**
Audio CD	**1-58659-269-6**
The Twin	1-58659-081-2
Cassette	1-58659-091-X
Audio CD	1-58659-268-8

Project Editor: Carol E. Newell
Cover Illustrator: Fujiko
Cover Design: Tony Amaro
©2004 Artesian Press

ISBN 1-58659-083-9

Chapter 1

"Mama!" Danica laughed. "Will you look at how dirty this table is? I can write my name in the dust!"

"We were lucky to find any place at all this late," Mom grumbled, staring at the ancient, musty furniture in the hotel room.

"Yeah," Dad agreed. "It was getting dark, and we're in the middle of the Great Smoky Mountains. Hear what I'm saying? It almost was sleeping in the car time!"

"Yeah, but this place is sure el dumpo," eleven year old Vernon said, peering out the cobwebbed window. "Man, I bet about a million spiders live here."

"Ugh!" Danica said. "Do we have to stay here?"

Just then they heard it, the long, throbbing howl. The Millers stared at one another. Danica thought it was an animal, but she'd never heard such a sound from any animal she'd ever seen.

"It's a ghost," Vernon cried, "somebody who died in this room and doesn't want us to stay!"

"Nonsense," Dad snapped.

"It's probably something perfectly ordinary," Mom said in a shaky voice.

"Mom, when we drove up here I saw a faded old sign—Dr. Benjamin Strubridge. I bet he was a mad scientist, and he had his laboratory here," Danica said.

"Yeah," Vernon chimed in, "some guy like that Dr. Frankenstein in the movies. He probably made monsters in the basement, and some of 'em are still here."

"Don't be ridiculous," Dad growled.

"This is a nice old hotel. That guy who signed us in was a perfect gentleman."

Danica hadn't liked the place when she first saw it. It was called the Iris Arms. It was a three story Victorian house converted to a hotel. Huge trees surrounded the house, and one was dead. Its leafless, wispy branches scratched the windows like the bony fingers of a skeleton! "This place just gives me the creeps," Danica said, hugging herself.

"You watch too much stupid TV," Dad said. "I'm tired. Let's just unpack and get some sleep. I've been driving for hours!"

"Your father is right," Mom said. "We all need a good night's sleep."

Vernon looked out the window. "Look, the moon looks like a big white beetle caught in the spider web branches of that old dead tree."

"Will you stop talking like that?" Dad said. "Let's get ready for bed, boy,

3

and make it snappy."

Vernon walked to the sofa bed he would use. "Bet there's spiders under the covers," he said.

"Enough!" Dad roared.

"Do you think that guy who signed us in was Dr. Strubridge?" Danica whispered to Vernon. He was a strange looking man with a round, bald head and little beady eyes that watered all the time behind huge glasses.

"Yeah," Vernon said. "Bet it was him all right. He looked like a mad scientist. I bet he's got a lab in the basement right now, and it's full of half-done monsters!"

Danica's eyes widened. "Maybe he lures in poor unsuspecting tourists like us, and they end up in the lab!" Danica recalled Dad turning off on a little used side road because Mom said it looked "enchanting". That was their fatal mistake. There would have been plenty of nice motels on the main highway.

4

"Danica, stop playing into your brother's silly notions," Mom said. "You're a teenager. I expect more from you!"

Danica opened her sofa bed and a cloud of dust rose up. "Ugh! I can see the moths flying around!" she complained.

"Danica ..." Mom began, but her voice stopped when the howl returned, louder, more tormented than before.

Chapter 2

"Mama!" Danica cried. "What in the world is that?"

"Lord have mercy," Mom said, "how should I know?"

Dad pulled on his bathrobe. "Well, I'm going to find out. We'd better get it settled that there's a noisy old hound downstairs if this family is ever going to get any sleep!"

"Be careful, Dad," Vernon said. "Some of the monsters Dr. Strubridge made might be roaming through the halls."

"There are no monsters, boy!" Dad thundered. He swung open the door and bounded downstairs with Danica and Vernon close behind. They all marched down the circular staircase to the lobby.

The bald man sat at his desk rummaging through a stack of papers. "Well, is everything all right in your room, folks?" he asked with a faint smile. He seemed like a very unhappy man. His smile wasn't cheerful.

"The room is okay," Dad said, "but that noise—it has my family upset."

"Noise? What noise?" asked the bald man.

"The howling," Danica said. "That unearthly howling from a beast or something."

The man smiled, revealing glittering gold-filled teeth. "Oh, you must mean Lucretia. I've gotten so used to her that I don't even notice her anymore."

"Who is Lucretia?" Dad asked grimly.

"A hyena. She lives in the mountains—sleeps in the daytime, but comes out at night and howls," the bald man said.

Danica and Vernon looked at each other. Danica looked the man in the eye and said, "Everybody knows hyenas don't live in the Great Smoky Mountains. They live in Africa and Asia."

"Of course, dear child," the man said with a flash of anger, "but this hyena, a large, ugly creature I dare say, escaped from some carnival a few years ago. Now it lurks in the wilderness. A real problem for nervous folks from the city like you."

"Well, now that we know what it is, we'll just ignore it," Dad said.

As the Millers went back upstairs, Danica said, "Do you believe what he said, Dad?"

"Of course. Why would he lie?" Dad asked.

"'Cause he's a mad scientist, and he wants to put us in his laboratory," Vernon said.

"Zip your lip, boy. I don't want to

hear any more nonsense," Dad said. "I'm going to bed and going to sleep. Lucretia can howl her head off for all I care."

Danica sprinted up the stairs ahead of the others. At school she was a track star. She was the first to tell Mom the hyena story.

"Well, bless my soul, now I've heard everything!" Mom laughed. "I just hope the giraffes and the elephants don't come next!"

Danica was the last in the family to go to sleep. Dad was asleep and snoring lightly. Even Vernon and Mom were drifting off as Danica went one last time to look from the window. She wondered if there was a runaway hyena out there. She thought if she looked long enough she might see the animal's burning eyes.

Danica had seen pictures of hyenas with their wide, ugly faces and their little round ears. She smiled to herself as she looked into the darkness. What a story she'd have to tell her friends back at school in Chicago—that she saw an African laughing hyena in the Great Smoky Mountains!

Danica gasped when she saw a shadow moving across the backyard of the hotel. It wasn't a hyena, it was a man. The bald man walked slowly to the Miller car. He looked around and up at the windows of their room. Danica shrank back behind the dusty curtains. "Nooo," Danica whispered as he opened the hood.

Chapter 3

"Mom! Dad!" Danica cried. "Come quick! That bald guy is messing with our car!"

Dad scrambled from bed, stubbing his toe. He hopped to the window, but by the time he got there, the bald man was gone and the hood was closed. "What? Where? What are you talking about, girl?"

"Dad, I saw that bald guy messing with our car!" Danica cried. "He did something to the engine!"

"You sure your eyes weren't playing tricks, Danica?" Dad demanded.

"I know what I saw!" Danica argued.

"Danica, when you get a crazy notion in your mind, you hang onto it like a dog with a bone. Now go to bed and let us all get some sleep, okay! It's going to be morning in a few hours, all bright and cheerful. We'll be getting a ham and eggs breakfast. The whole world is going to look different."

Danica finally went to bed. She wondered, was it possible she'd stared so long into the darkness that she did mistake a shadow for the bald man? Was her imagination maybe working overtime?

Danica laid in the sofa bed listening to the dead tree branches scratching the window, nagging at her. The old house creaked in all its joints. Danica had no problem picturing the heavy footsteps of some semi-human creature advancing towards their door. Every horror movie she ever saw came to her mind in gory detail. Finally, near dawn, Danica fell into a fitful sleep. When she awoke the sun was shining, and Dad was shaving.

"Remember just outside of town we saw this pancake house?" Dad was saying. "Let's double back and have our breakfast there. Boy, I can just taste some of those little round sausages with my pancakes."

"Hurrah," Vernon shouted, jumping from bed.

Everybody quickly dressed and headed downstairs.

"I'll do the driving to begin with," Mom said, sliding behind the wheel, "so you're not grumpy from being tired, Tyrone."

"Good idea, Babe," Dad said.

"Hey," Mom said, "why won't this car start?"

"Sure you're doin' it right?" Dad asked.

Mom rolled her eyes. "I've only been driving for twenty-two years! I'm telling you, Tyrone, it won't start!" she said.

"I told you he messed with the engine," Danica shrieked from the back seat. "He's got us trapped here!"

"Yeah!" Vernon shouted. "So he can do experiments on us!"

"Whoa!" Dad yelled. "Don't everybody go off half-cocked. I'll just pop the hood and see what I can see."

"Dad," Danica said, "you don't know a carburetor from a battery. You need Mom to add brake fluid!"

"Cool it, girl," Dad said, staring at the complicated array of wires and parts. Danica was right. He was an English teacher and knew every one of Shakespeare's sonnets, but he didn't know a thing about cars.

"Something wrong, folks?" asked the bald man who came strolling up.

"We can't start our car," Dad said. "Is there a garage around here?"

"Better than that. I'm pretty handy around engines. Let me have a look," the bald man said. He stuck his head under the hood. "Uh-oh," he said.

Danica blurted it out then. She knew it was stupid to confront him like this, but she did it anyway. "I saw you looking in our engine late last night. I was looking out the window, and I saw you messing with our car!"

The bald man turned slowly. He looked right at Danica. A sly smile danced on his thin lips. "My, you are an observant young lady. I'll bet you're very good in school. But sometimes when you see something, it's not exactly what you think you see."

Chapter 4

"It's true that I was looking at your engine, but when you folks pulled in last night I heard a strange sound coming from it. And I smelled something odd, like a part burning out. Well, I checked it out last night. But, sad to say, I didn't discover the problem. Now I have spotted it—you've got a burned out ignition system is what you've got," the bald man said.

"Oh, man," Dad said, "is that a big problem?"

"Well, yes and no. I'll have to call for a rebuilt part. Then I'll have it fixed in a couple of hours," the bald man said. "In the meantime, since you folks will be spending some extra time here,

I'll whip you up a mess of the best flapjacks you ever tasted."

"Sounds good," Mom said. "We'll pay you for the breakfast and the auto repairs."

"Well," the bald man said, "I can use the money. Time was, before they built the big highway, lots of tourists passed this way. Not no more. Now we get the leftovers, just a few folks looking for a scenic drive. Folks like you."

"Are you Doctor Strubridge?" Dad asked.

"Oh, mercy. No. That'd be my brother Benjamin. I'm Cyrus. You folks can just call me Cyrus," he said.

"Where is Doctor Strubridge?" Vernon asked.

"Vernon," Mom said, "don't ask personal questions."

"It's okay," Cyrus said. "My brother's been in Europe a long time. Left the place with me."

Danica watched Cyrus closely. His

eyes blinked rapidly every time he spoke, as if he was lying. Danica was sure that most everything he said was a lie.

"Benjamin, he was the big shot in the family, the genius," Cyrus said as he poured pancake batter into a sizzling iron pan on an ancient stove. "Trade school was good enough for me, but he went to medical school."

Danica noticed Cyrus' jaw worked when he talked about Benjamin. He didn't seem to like his brother much.

"My," Mom said, "these are lovely pancakes."

"Thank you, Mrs. Miller. I've worked as a fry cook, mechanic, you name it, I've done it. As Ben used to say 'jack of all trades and master of none'. He always enjoyed needling me, you know, how some brothers do." He laughed bitterly.

"Was your brother in practice here?" Mom asked.

"For a while ... had some ... ah ... mishaps. Went into research then. Looking for a cure from something afflicting mankind for centuries ... baldness." Cyrus tapped his own shiny head. "All the Strubridge men go bald at thirty-five. Ben was working on a miracle formula," his voice trailed off. "Well, better get to fixing your car."

As Cyrus worked on the engine, the Millers sat on the shady porch. "I don't care what you say," Danica told her parents, "something awful is going on here!"

"Don't be so suspicious," Mom said.

Danica and Vernon went inside the parlor to look at the books on the many shelves.

"Look at those dusty old books," Vernon sighed. "I bet if we took one down we'd sneeze our heads off."

"Vernon!" Danica whispered. "Do you hear like a rapping sound from down in the basement?"

"Yeah!" Vernon said, his eyes growing large.

"Maybe it's just the plumbing," Danica hoped.

Vernon took down a worn copy of *Treasure Island* and four insects scurried away. "Ugh!" Vernon said.

"There it is again," Danica said. "The rapping."

"Know what," Vernon said. "I think old Cyrus is Dr. Strubridge himself. And there's some poor creature in the basement that wants out!"

Chapter 5

Danica grabbed her brother's shoulders. "Vernon, what do you think he wants with us?"

"Maybe just to get money. Like he said, hardly anybody comes down the old road. Maybe like, he just needs money. Now that we're here he wants to get all he can from us."

Danica and Vernon went out on the porch where their parents sat. "Mama," Danica said, "something bad is going on in this place. I can feel it in my bones. Vern and I heard knocking sounds like somebody is trapped in the basement."

"Or some 'thing' is trapped down there," Vernon said. "Maybe one of his experiments that went bad."

"Here we go again," Dad said. "Probably old Cyrus is about done fixing the car, and we'll be on our way before lunchtime."

"You know," Mom said, "I heard that strange rapping, too. It was getting on my nerves."

"Could be just settling noises from the house," Dad said, frowning.

"But ... once or twice I was sure there was a pattern to the knocking," Mom said. "Like Morse code or something, like somebody was trying to send a message. I was sure I heard long and short sounds. Oh, I don't know...."

"Babe," Dad said. "you're letting the kids' imaginations get to you."

Mom reached out and placed a firm hand on Dad's arm, "Tyrone, I think the kids might be right. I'm really uneasy here. I think we'd better just call a cab and get out of here and send a garage back for the car."

"Well, if you really feel strongly," Dad said.

"Shhh!" Danica whispered. She saw a shadow around the side of the house. She was sure Cyrus—or whoever he was—was eavesdropping. Danica leaned close to her parents and whispered, "I think he's listening to us."

A look of real fear streaked through Mom's eyes.

"Tell you what," Dad whispered, "I'll just duck on inside and call a cab now. There's a phone by the front desk. You keep on talking in case he's listening."

Everybody nodded tensely. Danica and Vernon started talking about wanting to see the sights in the Great Smoky Mountains National Park. "I want to see the tulip tree that's almost two hundred feet high," Vernon said.

"I can't wait to see the deer, and I want to see those blueberries and huckleberries."

"I hope we see a bobcat," Vernon said.

Dad returned, looking worried for the first time since they'd come here. "Phone's out," he muttered.

"Oh, no!" Mom gasped. "Now I am scared. He must have heard us talking and cut the wires!"

Danica stared down the long lane they'd followed when they saw the sign *Iris Arms—reasonable rates*. The hotel was about a fourth of a mile off the scenic road which was, itself, isolated. How she longed to see the busy main highway again. People just didn't come this way very often. How would they get help?

Suddenly Cyrus appeared. "Well, folks, we've got a small problem. Looks like you'll have to spend another night here. My parts man said he couldn't get the rebuilt until tomorrow morning. The car won't move without it."

"Did you know the phone is out?"

Dad said.

"Oh, she'll go out like that from time to time. We don't worry about it out here. We don't lead such a rushed life that we can't wait for a phone to get fixed," Cyrus said. His small eyes glittered. "Say, I'll be needing cash for the parts man tomorrow. Could you give me a couple hundred right now?"

Danica watched her father dole out two hundred dollars. Cyrus smiled and folded the money, shoving it in his pocket. "Money sure is nice, ain't it? I always dreamed of being rich one day. Still do. Oh, you folks might hear a rapping sound. That'd be woodpeckers at the dead wood ... whole house is dead wood, I reckon. Sorta makes the house like a tomb, don't it?" He laughed with an awful, cackling sound.

Chapter 6

"Oh, and another thing," Cyrus said, "I told you about Lucretia. Well, hyenas can be real mean. Don't want to scare you, but it'd be best if you folks stayed inside, specially at night."

"I'm not afraid of hyenas," Dad said.

"Well, maybe you ought to be, Mr. Miller. They're big—six feet long—weigh as much as a man. For all I know maybe other hyenas escaped with Lucretia. Might be a pack out there. If they see a human, why they run them down. They're hunters, don't you know...." Cyrus opened his long, black coat revealing a pistol stuck in his belt. "That's why I keep this handy. I know how to use it, too."

Danica felt cold chills go up her spine. She figured Cyrus was showing them the gun for another reason—to scare them.

"If I was to see anything moving in the night," Cyrus continued, "why I'd be liable to fire away. Be a terrible thing if I'd haul off and shoot one of you folks, thinking you were hyenas. That's why you best stay inside."

"I see," Mom said tightly.

Cyrus smiled. "Yes, ma'am, that's good. I had you figured for a smart lady. Tell me, what do you do in Chicago?"

"I teach Chemistry in high school," Mom said.

Cyrus slapped his thigh, raising dust. "If that don't just beat all! I can tell smart folks. I guess that's from growing up with a smart brother. Folks were always saying how smart he was and how dumb I was. Ben and his friends had a rhyme about it. 'Cy, Cy, got to the brain well after Ben had drunk it dry'." Cyrus' laughter was a dry, angry crackle like someone stomping on crispy fall leaves.

When the Millers were alone in their room, Dad said, "We've got to play it cool. I don't know what's goin' on here, but we'd better not push Cyrus into taking desperate action. Tomorrow I'll give him the rest of the cash and tell him that's all we've got. I figure he'll get the car started then and send us on our way."

"You mean we've got to spend another night here?" Danica groaned.

"I don't want to either," Vernon said.

"I say we just wait until dark and just start walking down the road," Danica said. "I'm sure we'll come to a farmhouse in about two miles."

Dad looked at Mom. "What do you think, Babe?"

"I'm with the kids," Mom said. "I'm so scared I can't bear to spend another night here. Let's wait until around ten and then just go for it. We'll sneak out the back way. Cyrus will probably be asleep."

"Okay," Dad said, "if everybody feels that way, but it'll be risky."

Danica couldn't wait until the sun began to go down. All through dinner as they ate beef stew cooked by Cyrus, Danica was thinking about making a break for it. Danica and Vernon talked about all the interesting things they'd already seen on the vacation. Maybe Cyrus would feel secure so he'd be sleeping tight when they escaped tonight.

"Did your brother ever find that cure for baldness, Cyrus?" Dad asked after supper as they all sat on the porch.

Cyrus nodded. "Yes, he did. I loaned him some of my savings for what he called the experimental trials … my own hard earned cash. I gave it to him, and then he said he had the formula just right except for one or two small details."

Danica and Vernon looked at each other. If Doctor Strubridge had the cure for baldness how come Cyrus was still bald? Or was it all just a crazy lie?

Cyrus turned to them then. "He wouldn't share it. After all I'd done for him, he wanted to keep it all for himself." Cyrus' voice shook with pure hatred. "He wouldn't share."

Chapter 7

"Share what?" Dad asked, keeping his voice calm even though Danica could tell her father was scared.

"The formula. Always said we'd be partners, he swore it." Cyrus shook his head. "Greed does awful things to people. Well, sun's going down now and time to turn in. We'll leave the night to Lucretia and her pack. Don't want to be meeting up with those sharp-toothed customers."

The Millers went up the winding staircase to their room and closed the door. Then they waited. Cyrus made noises walking around downstairs for a while. Finally, around 10:30, there was silence. They waited about thirty minutes more so he'd be sound asleep.

Danica peered out the window. There was a light wind and the sky was filled with dark-edged clouds. The moon was hiding. That was good. A moonless night was better for hiding in.

"Let's go," Dad said. "Follow me, everybody and be as quiet as possible." Danica nodded, glancing at Vernon. Usually Vernon was making wisecracks, even in tough times, but now his face was taut.

Dad opened the door slowly, and they walked down the hall on the moldy carpet. Each step seemed to make a loud creak no matter how carefully they moved. The old floor beneath the carpet was half rotted. They moved down the circular staircase, then turned towards the back door. It was locked from the inside and they opened it, making another grating squeak. Everybody winced. Danica thought her heart would stop from pure terror. But Cyrus didn't appear. Dad swung the door wide. The darkness welcomed them, and the cool night air felt good on their faces. Hope surged through Danica's heart. She thought they'd make it now.

As they walked along the side of the house, beside tiny basement windows, Danica gasped. A human hand groped at the air beyond the tiny window.

"Mama! Dad!" Danica cried. "There's somebody down there in the basement!"

"Come on!" Dad commanded. They began to run, stumbling, scrambling to get on the driveway and then down to the country road and civilization.

"Hold it!" Came a voice as sharp as a pistol shot. Cyrus stood there, gun in hand. "Don't you folks see Lucretia out there ahead of you? And her pack is with her ... eyes glowing, don't you know ..."

Danica saw nothing but the darkness.

"Best you get back inside, folks, before you get hurt," Cyrus said.
"Lucretia and her pack, they're going
for a kill tonight."

Dad took Danica's hand and Mom
took Vernon's. They walked back inside
the old hotel, their spirits sinking.
Cyrus followed them inside, gun still in
hand.

"Close call, eh?" Cyrus said with a
twisted smile. "Wasn't very smart of
you folks to go poking around like that.
If I hadn't of come along, why Lucretia
and the pack would be having a mid-
night snack of you right now."

Cyrus took a whisky bottle down
from the cupboard and took a long,
deep swig. "Just the thing to settle the
nerves, don't you know? Don't like to
be coming on Lucretia in the dead of
night, no siree."

Dad gave Danica's hand a reassur-
ing squeeze, but it didn't help much.

Danica couldn't remember ever being so scared in her life. Mom had her arm around Vernon.

Cyrus took another drink and wiped his mouth. "Mr. Miller, you're a lucky man to have a boy and a girl, don't you know. Two boys, brothers, you got problems. Like Ben and me. He was always trying to make life miserable for me, and he was smart enough to know all the ways, too. Then I invested in his scheme anyway and didn't he turn on me like a snake." Cyrus' little eyes narrowed then. "You were sneaking off, weren't you?" he said bitterly. "That's what you were doing?"

Chapter 8

"We're running out of money," Dad explained, "And we have to be back to work soon. We just figured we'd hike to town and catch a bus to Chicago, send a garage back for the car."

Cyrus grinned over his gold teeth. "I was a fool in the old days. I believed smooth talk."

"No, Cyrus, no jive. We just want to go home," Dad said.

"So, how much money you got left?" Cyrus asked.

Dad opened his wallet. "A hundred and twenty and some change."

"Well, I think you owe me at least that," Cyrus said.

"Fine," Dad said, handing over the

money.

Cyrus counted the bills carefully. "I've been fleeced by plenty of folks, usually nice, smart folks like you. No offense, but a man like me has had to fight for what little he's got. I woulda been rich if only Ben had shared like he promised. Had the formula written down, ready to go into production ... wouldn't share it with me." Cyrus shook his head.

"Now that we've settled accounts," Dad said, "why don't we just walk on to town tonight without putting you out anymore, Cyrus."

"No. Wouldn't want it on my conscience if Lucretia and her pack ate you up tonight. You better spend the night and leave when it's daybreak. You paid for two nights, and you'd better take 'em." Cyrus said.

When the Millers were back in their room, Danica felt panicky. "Dad, he's not going to let us go ever, and you know it!"

"We're doomed," Vernon said, "like that thing in the basement, that poor monster with his claw sticking out the grated window! That was probably once a poor tourist like us!"

"Take it easy," Dad said. "Cyrus is drinking tonight. Maybe he'll drink so much that he'll go into a really deep sleep. We can make another break for it before dawn."

"I bet the basement is full of tourists like us who never left the Iris Arms," Vernon cried.

"We've got to keep our heads," Mom said.

Danica looked at her parents. "I've got an idea. One of us has got to escape, and not down the stairs where Cyrus is probably watching. I mean out the window and down the fire escape."

"I'll go," Vernon said.

"No," Danica said, "you're too young. I'm the best hope we've got. I can climb. When I'm on the ground I can run. I set the record at school for the fastest mile ever run by a girl. I could get help in no time at all."

"But, honey, it'd be dangerous," Mom said.

"Staying here is more dangerous," Danica said. "Mom, it's our only chance. He's not going to let us go. Please, Mom, Dad, let me try. Traveling alone I could reach that farmhouse and call the police in maybe fifteen minutes."

Danica's father took her in his arms and hugged her. "Baby, I've been looking after you for almost sixteen years. It's sure a funny feeling to ask you to do something risky for the rest of us."

Danica kissed her father's cheek. "I gotta go, Dad, for all of us!"

"Go with God, baby," Mom whispered.

Danica climbed from the window and moved slowly down the rusted old fire escape. The ground looked very far below, and Danica knew that one slip and she could break her leg or her neck. Then they'd really all be finished.

As Danica climbed, she heard the soft howling coming from the poor creature in the basement. Once Danica reached a phone she could help him, too.

Danica reached the bottom of the fire escape. Then she swung over to a porch rail and dropped to the ground.

From out of nowhere, Cyrus sprang up behind her, pulling a potato sack over her head.

Chapter 9

Cyrus clamped his hand over Danica's mouth and dragged her down into the basement. He pushed her through a door and slammed it after her, leaving her in total darkness. From outside the locked room, Cyrus snarled, "It's your own fault. I can't let you go. You'll send the police, and I'll never get the formula. I'll never be rich and living the good life!"

As Danica's eyes grew accustomed to the darkness she saw the little wizened man who huddled in rags in the corner. "W-who are you?" she asked.

"Doctor Benjamin Strubridge," the old man whimpered. "I have been wrongfully imprisoned here by my evil brother for almost a year!"

"But why?" Danica asked.

"The formula. For decades I've been looking for a formula to cure baldness. I almost had it. I came here to ask Cyrus for a bit more money to complete my work, but he went mad! Insisted I already had the formula and wouldn't share it with him! We had a terrible fight, and he overpowered me and dragged me down here."

Danica stared around the small cell-like room. She had failed herself and—what was worse—her family. Now they were probably all doomed. Dad would never get back to his English class, or Mom to her Chemistry lab. Vernon wouldn't get to play Little League baseball. She would never see her friends back in Chicago again. Danica began to cry.

"I'm so sorry, young lady," the little man said. "It's all so sad. He rented to tourists to make money. Tried to fleece them, but this is the worst. He's growing madder! Oh, it's all my fault. I promised him our lives would turn to gold when I had the formula. It's all greed! Greed!"

Danica stared at the broken man she pitied so much, and she forgot her own fear. Why was she wasting her time crying when she could be using her brains? "Dr. Strubridge, what if you did have the formula, would he let you go?" she asked.

"You don't understand," Dr. Strubridge said. "I don't have it."

"But you could tell him you have it," Danica said.

"What?" the man gasped.

"Yes! Say you are finally ready to share it," Danica said.

"But ... but ..." the man stammered, confused.

"Just follow my lead, Dr. Strubridge," Danica said.

She pounded on the door until Cyrus came.

"What's the racket?" Cyrus demanded.

"Your brother has decided to share the formula," Danica said. "I talked him into it."

Cyrus held the pistol in his hand as he opened the door. "Benjamin! Is it true?" he asked.

"Yes, yes," Dr. Strubridge muttered.

"Tell me where you hid the formula," Cyrus said. "It's in this house, isn't it?" Cyrus' eyes were frantic. "I always knew it was in this house."

"He said it's in the library," Danica said. Inside she was shaking with fear but on the outside she had turned to steel. She felt strangely powerful, in charge. "I'll show you where. He told me."

"How devilishly clever, Benjamin," Cyrus screamed. "You hid it in a book thinking I was too stupid to read books so your secret would be safe."

"I'll show you just where it is," Danica said. "He can't remember the exact book, but he described the cover. I remember seeing a cover like that when I was looking for a book to read yesterday...."

"All right, march! The two of you," Cyrus hissed, "and if we don't find the formula I'll feed you both to Lucretia tonight!"

Chapter 10

Danica wished she could get word to her parents that she was okay, but that was out of the question. One small mistake and her plan was ruined.

Danica strode to the bookcase and took down *Treasure Island.* The shocked and frightened doctor watched her in wonder and confusion. He didn't have a clue about what Danica was doing.

With trembling fingers Danica flipped through the book, glancing at the open door that led into the darkness. "Aha," she said, her fingers closing over a tattered bookmark that said *I fell asleep here.* "Here is the formula, all written down."

"Give it to me," Cyrus shouted,

groping for the bookmark he thought was the formula.

Danica had just one chance—to pretend she had the secret formula and to run with it. Her pride and her school's pride depended on her sprints to the finish line. This time lives were at stake.

Danica hurled the book into Cyrus' startled face, staggering him and knocking his glasses off. Then she burst into a desperate sprint for the door, still clutching the bookmark. In a few precious seconds Cyrus had recovered his glasses. He was in pursuit, pistol in hand. "Stop!" he screamed. "Come back! Do you hear me? Come back!"

Cyrus seemed right behind Danica, but she had made it into the woods that marched alongside the driveway. The moon was still lost behind the storm clouds that would bring rain by dawn. Danica was thankful for that. It was harder for Cyrus to see her as she raced through the trees.

Danica kicked a stone, and it struck her ankle, gashing her. She felt the blood running into her sock, but she never slowed her pace. She remembered those crucial track meets at school with all her friends yelling, "Go, Dani, go," but they were nothing compared to this.

"The hyenas are coming, " Cyrus screamed in a croaking voice. Danica never slowed or even looked back. She knew the hyenas were a lie like everything the miserable, greedy man said. No wild beasts tracked her—only a man so driven by greed that he was worse than any beast.

Danica ran on, her chest aching mercilessly. Cyrus was old, and he couldn't keep up, but at some point would he get a clear shot at her? If he did, she couldn't outrun a bullet. Danica knew if she tossed down the bookmark he would stop chasing her, but then he'd soon discover he'd been tricked. He'd double back to the house and take revenge on her parents and Vernon. So she ran on, darting through the trees, ignoring his curses and threats.

At last Danica saw the road in the distance with a farmhouse and a small gas station on the corner. A pay phone stood there. Danica looked back and screamed, "Here's your old formula!" She tossed it into a thicket and ran into the pay phone booth and dialed 911.

Cyrus dove into the thicket in search of what he thought was the formula. He clawed at weeds and mud until at last his fingers closed around the piece of paper.

She heard Cyrus' scream of despair when he found he'd been duped—that the paper was only a bookmark. It was the most horrifying howl that Danica had ever heard. But it mixed with the wails of arriving police sirens. Danica had won the race of her life.

After the police took Cyrus away, another Sergeant drove Danica back to the Iris Arms. She leaped out into the arms of her parents.

"Oh, baby," Dad said, giving her a bear hug, "you're a hero!"

"A super hero!" Vernon agreed.

Before the ambulance drove off with Dr. Benjamin Strubridge, the frail old man offered Danica his hand. "You saved my life," he whispered. "Bless you, young lady. I'll never forget you!"

A mechanic from town got the Miller car running in short order and soon the family was on the road again. They were crossing Kentucky and heading for the Ohio River as dusk gathered.

"Chicago, here we come!" Vernon shouted. "I can't wait to play baseball again with the Maple Street Tigers!"

"I can't wait to tell my friends everything that happened," Danica said. "Let them try to match my story!"

"Slow down," Mom commanded, spotting a bed and breakfast inn set back among the trees. "Wouldn't that be a cozy place to spend the night?"

"Looks like the Iris Arms!" Vernon shouted.

"It looks worse than that!" Danica shrieked.

"It looks enchanting," Mom insisted.

Dad threw up his hands helplessly as they drove towards the inn in the shadowy twilight.

From a nearby lake, a loon could be heard laughing in the darkness.